JAN. 1 3 1994

Earthquake in the Third Grade

By LAURIE MYERS

Illustrated by KAREN RITZ

Clarion Books
New York

Clarion Books
a Houghton Mifflin Company imprint
215 Park Avenue South, New York, NY 10003
Text copyright © 1993 by Laurie Myers
Illustrations copyright © 1993 by Karen Ritz

Printed in the U.S.A.

Library of Congress Cataloging-in-Publication Data

Myers, Laurie.
Earthquake in the third grade / by Laurie Myers ; illustrated by Karen Ritz.
p.   cm.
Summary: Just as the ants feel a jolt when John knocks over the ant farm,
John and his third grade classmates find their world turned upside down
following the news of their beloved teacher's imminent departure.
ISBN 0–395–65360–6
[1. Teachers—Fiction.   2. Schools—Fiction.]   I. Ritz, Karen, ill.   II. Title.
PZ7.M9873Ear   1993
[E]—dc20
92-26609   CIP   AC

BP   10   9   8   7   6   5   4   3   2   1

For my parents Ed and Betsy Byars

—L. M.

*For Andy and his third-grade friends
at Nativity School*

—K. R.

Contents

CHAPTER 1

An Act of John Jacobs

No one stopped for a break. No one stopped to eat. They kept going. Each one concentrated on the job. They carried their heavy loads from one pile to another, back and forth, crawling in and out of tunnels.

There was not a sound. Occasionally two workers would pause beside each other. They would touch as if giving a high five. Then they would continue working.

The work was going well. They had started two weeks ago when they were, unwillingly, dumped here. Now the pile of sand was getting bigger. The tunnels were getting longer. Everyone was pleased, even the leader, who continued working right alongside the others.

Although the leader didn't know it, his every move was being studied. There was no way he could have known this. And there was no way he could know about the big disaster that was about to occur.

A worker followed the leader to the top of the green plastic barn. They paused there. It was at this moment that it happened.

An act of God, that's what people call an earthquake. But this earthquake was not an act of God. It was an act of John Jacobs.

"Mom!" John cried when it happened. "I knocked over the ant farm!"

His mother appeared in the doorway at once. "They didn't get out, did they?"

"No. I was reaching for my bookbag and look!"

Chaos had replaced order in the ant community. The leader and his crew had been thrown around. Some were buried under piles of sand. Some were trapped in tunnels. All were confused.

"Two weeks of work, destroyed! Sand everywhere. Tunnels gone." John's face dropped as he watched the ants run wildly over the grains of sand.

"Well, you can't do anything about it now. You have to catch the bus."

"Mom . . ."

"The bus is here!"

John stood the ant farm back up and ran out the door.

The ride to school was not a happy one. John dreaded breaking the news to his best friend Buzzy. Buzzy loved the ant farm. He wanted one of his own. In fact, he had gotten one for his birthday last year, but his mother had given it away.

"I don't want any animals I can't see without my glasses," she had said.

"That narrows it down to elephants," Buzzy had told John.

When John got to school, Buzzy was waiting in the doorway.

"Did they make it to the top?" he asked eagerly.

"No," John answered. He walked straight to his desk. He avoided looking at Kate, who sat behind him. He liked her, but she always wanted to know everything.

Buzzy followed John. "I was sure they would

be at the top by now. What happened?" Buzzy asked.

John kicked his bookbag under the desk. "I knocked it over," he said.

Buzzy gasped and sank into his own seat beside John.

"Knocked what over?" Kate asked.

"My ant farm."

Kate sighed. "Is that all? Just some old ants?"

Buzzy straightened, like a soldier ready for battle. "They are not 'some old ants.' They are . . . they are . . . individuals," he said, proud to have found the perfect word.

Buzzy leaned toward Kate, his face serious. "There is one with a little head. I call him Pea Brain. And there's one that stays in the lowest chamber and digs all the time. He's Digger. And two of them follow Big Jim."

"Big Jim?" Kate asked.

"Yeah. He's the leader."

Kate rolled her eyes in John's direction.

"We named him after my uncle," John said defensively.

"John's uncle is huge," Buzzy added.

"Well, I hope you haven't told your uncle that you named an insect after him. I mean, insects aren't the cutest things in the world. And if your uncle is as big as you say, and he didn't like the idea . . ." Her voice trailed off.

John grinned. "There's one ant with a big mouth. We're thinking of calling her Kate."

Kate reached over and swung at John. She missed. Buzzy laughed.

"How far did the ants get, John?" asked Buzzy.

"About halfway to the top. Plus, they had started a new tunnel."

"Ooooooooh," Buzzy groaned at the thought of the ant labor he would never see. He shook his head. "You never know when disaster is going to strike. You just never know."

CHAPTER 2

Disaster Strikes

"**B**efore we go to recess I have something to tell you," Mrs. Lucas began. She was using her serious voice. It was the same one she used when she told them the janitor had died. Everyone was quiet.

"Most of you know my husband, Captain Lucas, is in the army."

She was leaning against her desk.

For support, John thought. It must be bad news.

Mrs. Lucas looked at the class.

John braced himself for an earthquake.

"On Friday he received orders transferring him to a base in Texas," she said. "We will be moving this weekend."

No one spoke. Kate raised her hand.

"Yes, Kate?"

"Does this mean you are leaving?"

John cringed. Kate had the loudest voice at Whiteside Elementary. The volume of her voice made the news more real.

"Yes, Kate. Thursday will be my last day at school."

"Thursday?" Kate blurted out. "Why so soon?" Kate could be a pest, but at this moment she was speaking for everyone.

"Captain Lucas has a special assignment. He has to start on a project in Texas next Monday."

Tuesday, Wednesday, Thursday, John thought. Only three more days with Mrs. Lucas. He let out a sigh. She was his favorite teacher. Everyone in the school said that third grade was the best year because you had Mrs. Lucas for your teacher. They were right.

"Mr. Cunningham will be your new teacher," Mrs. Lucas said. "He'll be here on Friday."

"Mister?" John said out loud. "A man teacher?"

"Yes, John," Mrs. Lucas answered in the same calm voice she always used, "and I am certain that you are going to like him."

Mrs. Lucas was usually right about things. John was not convinced, however.

"I thought we would have a party on Thursday," Mrs. Lucas continued.

"A party?" John whispered to Buzzy. "Can you believe it? A party!"

"Yeah, some party that'll be."

John nodded. "What a day. First the ant farm, now this."

"The ant farm! What exactly did it look like?" Buzzy asked. "I mean after the earthquake."

"A mess."

"How about the main tunnel?"

"Gone."

"The side tunnels?"

"Gone."

"The little rooms?"

"Filled with sand."

Buzzy took a deep breath. "What about the ants?"

"They were in shock," John said. "It was kind of like this." He spread out his arms to take in the entire classroom.

Buzzy looked around. No one was working. They all hurried back and forth, busying themselves with activities that were familiar—sharpening pencils, going to the bathroom, getting a drink of water.

"I see what you mean," Buzzy said.

Kate leaned forward. "I can't believe it," she whispered.

John didn't say anything.

"It's just terrible!" she said.

"I know," John and Buzzy said together.

"We can't let her go, we just can't," Kate said. "And we won't."

Something in Kate's voice made the boys turn around. They looked at her curiously. Then Kate whispered four words—the only good words they had heard all day.

"I have a plan."

CHAPTER 3

The Letter

"**D**o you really think she has a plan?" Buzzy said on the way to Kate's house.

"I don't know," John answered. "She said she had a plan and to meet at her house."

"Well, I don't know how anyone can keep another person from moving." Buzzy kicked a rock. "Do you really think she has a plan?" he asked for the fourth time.

"You know Kate," John said.

"It better be a good one," Buzzy said. He caught up with the rock and kicked it again. "Because I haven't even seen the ant farm since the earthquake."

"You haven't missed anything."

"Haven't missed anything? How can you say

that? I have missed exactly . . ." Buzzy looked at his watch. "Seven hours of post-earthquake action."

He gave the rock a final kick.

"Let's handle one disaster at a time," John said.

Kate was waiting for them on the front steps of her house.

"So what's the plan?" Buzzy got right to the point.

"Mr. Lucas," Kate said firmly. "That's the plan."

"Who?" Buzzy asked.

"Her husband, mushbrain," said Kate in an irritated voice.

"Why?" Buzzy asked.

"Because he's the source of the problem, mushbrain."

Buzzy made a face. Kate was a master at name-calling. She could pick the worst name and make it stick—like Mustard Mouth for Andrew Wiley. He never wiped his mouth. And Big Foot for Mr. Dillard, the principal. He was always closing doors with his foot.

Buzzy still did not see the point, but he didn't

dare ask again. Mushbrain might become his name for the rest of the year.

"We need to go straight to the source of the problem," Kate explained. "Mr. Lucas."

"So what's the plan?" John asked.

"This is the plan," she said. She leaned closer, as if she were revealing a national secret.

"We write him a letter and explain just how important it is for Mrs. Lucas to stay."

John looked thoughtful. "That might work."

"So let's get started," Kate said. She pulled out a spiral notebook and started writing.

"Deeeer . . . Misssterrrr . . . Luuuuucas . . ." She read the words as she wrote them.

"Isn't he a captain or a general or something?" John asked.

Kate looked irritated by the interruption.

"It's Captain," Buzzy said firmly. He was pleased to know something that Kate didn't know.

Buzzy looked over Kate's shoulder at what she had written. "And it's d - e - *a* - r, not d - e - *e* - r," he said.

She looked critically at her paper. She didn't like making mistakes. She made an *a* out of the *e*.

"Mushbrain," he added with a grin.

When they finished the letter, Kate read it out loud.

Dear Captain Lucas,
Please don't take Mrs. Lucas to Texas. We need her. Our future depends on it. Also, there is a man teacher coming and we don't want him. Mrs. Lucas is the best teacher we ever had.
Love,
Kate, John, and
Buzzy

"I like it," Kate said. She stuck it in an envelope and handed it to Buzzy.

"Why are you giving it to me?"

"I did the writing; you deliver."

"I don't know where they live," Buzzy said. He felt uneasy.

John said, "It's the green house on Woodhill Road. We can put it in their mailbox on the way home."

"I hope this works," Kate said. "It's our only hope."

CHAPTER 4

Digger and Pea Brain Make Contact

Big Jim carried an ant leg to the top of the refuse pile. The pile was filled with sand, old food, and pieces of dead ants. It was on the top of the farm, well away from the tunnels and chambers that the workers were rebuilding.

"Digger is cleaning out the room at the bottom," Buzzy said. His face was only inches away from the side of the farm. "And get this. Pea Brain is busy digging toward him. There is only a half inch of sand between them and they don't even know it."

John lay on his bed looking at a comic book. He turned the pages without reading the words.

"I can't believe the earthquake was just this morning," Buzzy said. "Can you imagine how it

would feel to have your whole world turned upside down?"

He stood up and held his arms out like an ant. He fell sideways onto the floor and made a high-pitched cry. "EEEEEEEEEEEK." He lay on the floor moving his legs back and forth in a walking motion, pretending to walk sideways on the furniture.

"I know exactly how they feel," John said. "Our classroom had an earthquake today too."

Buzzy was now crawling sideways around the room. "We sure did!" he said. "Our science book says that animal life and human life can be alike. If they have earthquakes, then we can too."

John sat up on his bed. "Remember when we first got the ants and we were trying to get them into the farm?"

Buzzy laughed. "As soon as you took the stopper off of the mailing tube they started crawling up your arm."

"I was trying to shake them into the farm," John said. "They were all over the place. It was like the first day of school when everybody is running around trying to find their room."

Buzzy was still sideways. He worked his way back to the ant farm.

"Digger and Pea Brain are still digging," he reported. "They should make contact in one minute."

John tossed aside his comic book and hurried over to the ant farm.

"Go Digger go," Buzzy said softly. Digger's legs dug into the sand, pulling the grains down under him.

John started a countdown. "Ten, nine, eight . . ."

"Wait," Buzzy said. "Pea Brain is leaving to carry off sand."

They waited patiently as Pea Brain placed the sand in another pile and then quickly made his way back to the digging site.

John and Buzzy continued together. "Seven, six, five . . ."

"Stop," John said. "Digger is cleaning himself."

Digger rubbed his antennae through the comb on his foreleg. He started digging again.

"Four, three . . ."

The pieces of sand between the ants began to crumble.

"Two, one . . . contact!"

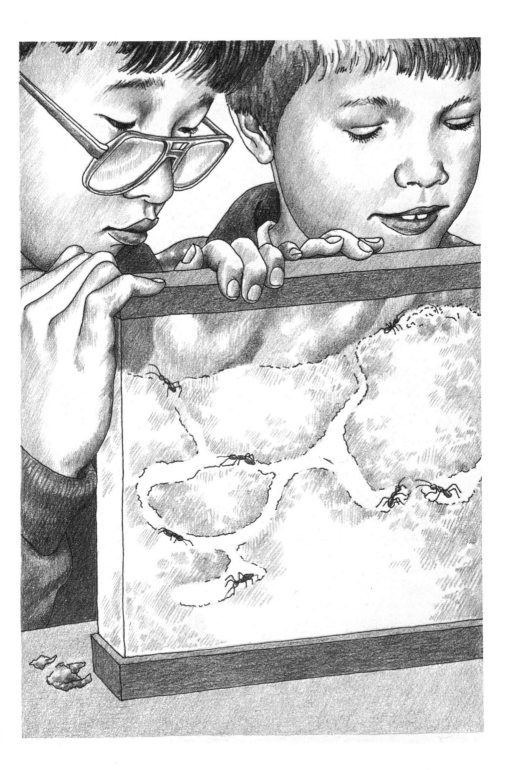

Digger and Pea Brain touched antennae through the small hole.

Buzzy smiled. "I think they might recover after all."

John nodded. "I bet they're hungry after all that work."

"Let's drop relief supplies to the victims," Buzzy said.

John opened the desk drawer and pulled a cornflake out of a plastic bag.

"Only half," Buzzy reminded him.

John pulled the plastic top off of the ant farm and dropped half of the cornflake inside. It landed on a pile of sand between two ants. They immediately began inspecting the food.

"Maybe somebody will drop us a relief package," Buzzy said.

John sighed. "Instead of a relief package, we're getting a man teacher. Can you believe it?"

"Yeah, I can believe it."

"We've never had a man teacher," John said. He and Buzzy had been in the same class since first grade.

"What's so terrible about a man teacher?" Buzzy asked, watching the ants sniff the cornflake. "My sister had Mr. Wren for fourth grade. From the very first day she complained about him. But at the end of the year she cried because she didn't want to leave him."

"I don't know," John said. "It's just different. That's all."

"So?"

"I like things to stay the same. Like the ants. The book said that they don't like change. I don't either."

"Well, if our letter works," Buzzy said, "there won't be a change."

"We'll find out tomorrow."

CHAPTER 5

A Dangerous Plan

Wednesday. In the ant farm the main tunnel was clear, and the side tunnels were being repaired. Things were not going as well at school. John knew it as soon as Mrs. Lucas called their names.

"John, Buzzy, Kate. I want to see you before recess."

The three friends exchanged glances. As the other children hurried out the door they slowly made their way to the front of the room.

Mrs. Lucas came around to the front of her desk. She was so close that John could smell her perfume. He took a deep breath.

Mrs. Lucas got right to the point. "The letter that you wrote to Mr. Lucas was very nice. I felt very special that you care that much about me."

"It's true," Kate said. It was the shortest sentence John had ever heard her say.

"Thank you," Mrs. Lucas said. "You know I still have to go to Texas."

John glanced at the others. Kate's eyes were on Mrs. Lucas. Buzzy was looking at the floor. They both looked disappointed. But John wasn't. He was thinking.

Before they left, Mrs. Lucas hugged each of them.

The walk to the playground gave John time to finish thinking. When they got there he turned to the others and said, "I have a plan."

Kate's face brightened. Her eyes opened wide. "What?" she asked.

"I brought a backup plan with me in case the letter didn't work."

"What is it?" Kate demanded.

"My plan is right here," he said, patting his pocket. "I don't have time to explain. We have to get inside the teachers' lounge."

Buzzy gulped. "The teachers' lounge? Are you crazy? Students aren't allowed in the teachers' lounge."

"I know," John said.

"And what about teachers?" Buzzy's voice got louder. "There might be teachers in there. After all, it is a *teachers'* lounge."

Kate sighed loudly. "Buzzy, you know the third grade teachers have recess duty, and the rest of the teachers are in class by now."

"You have to take a chance," John said. "If you want to be in on my plan, we have to sneak in now. Recess will be over in five minutes."

Buzzy was silent. He didn't like getting into trouble. And this seemed like it could be big trouble.

Kate's eyes twinkled. "I'm in," she said.

Buzzy rubbed his neck. Kate's response had really put the pressure on him.

"What if Mrs. Washburn is in there?" Buzzy asked slowly.

Kate placed her hands on her hips. "Don't be a chicken, Buzzy. Just because she is twice as mean as the other teachers . . ."

"And twice as big," Buzzy interrupted.

"Doesn't mean we can't sneak into the lounge," Kate finished. "Come on. Either you're in or you're out. What's it going to be?"

John watched Buzzy's face. He could tell Buzzy was thinking, probably about Mrs. Lucas and how she always made you feel like you could do anything.

"I'm in."

CHAPTER 6

No Students Allowed

John opened the school door. "The coast is clear," he said.

"Let's go," Kate said.

Suddenly Buzzy felt like the cowardly lion in the Wizard of Oz. He wished he had a tail to twist nervously in his hands. He knew exactly what he would say. "I do believe in Mrs. Washburn. I do believe in Mrs. Washburn. I do believe in Mrs. Washburn."

The three friends stepped quietly inside. Halfway down the hall they could see the door to the teachers' lounge. It was right across from the principal's office.

They started slowly and cautiously toward the door. They walked single file, like ants. John was in front, Kate next; Buzzy was last. Buzzy kept looking over his shoulder. The last thing he wanted was for Mrs. Washburn to sneak up on him. She always wore tennis shoes. He imagined her sneaking quietly behind him and suddenly yelling in his ear, "What do you think you're doing?"

ALL

There was a sign on the lounge door:
NO STUDENTS ALLOWED
Buzzy read it out loud.

Kate ignored him. "Mr. Dillard's office looks empty," she whispered.

"I wish the teachers' lounge had a glass door too," John said. "So we could see if there's anyone inside." He leaned toward the closed door listening for voices.

"Well, I don't hear anything." John took a deep breath. "Here goes." He pushed the door open a couple of inches and looked inside.

"The coast is clear," he said. "Buzzy, you stand guard while Kate and I go in. Knock if anybody comes."

Buzzy nodded. He rubbed his neck. Kate and John slipped into the lounge.

"What are we looking for?" Kate asked.

John's eyes scanned the room. In one corner there was a sofa and a snack machine. In the other there was a row of boxes, and a door that said RESTROOM.

"There it is," John said.

"The restroom?"

"No, the teachers' boxes. That's where they get their mail."

"So what's the plan?" Kate asked.

"This." He pulled a piece of paper out of his pocket.

She grabbed it.

"A blank sheet of paper?" she screamed. "This is what I risked my life for? A blank sheet of paper?"

John snatched the paper and turned it over.

"Oh," she said when she saw something was typed on the other side. She read the words aloud.

```
Dear Mr. Dillard,

We would like to nominate Mrs.
Lucas for Teacher-of-the-Year
Award.

                    John
Jacobs
                    Buzzy
Griffin
                    Kate
Walters

 P.S.Please notify her immediately
that she must stay in order to win
this award.
```

"Well," John said hopefully.

"It certainly looks official," Kate said.

"Do you think it will work?" John asked.

"Well," Kate said. "The award is for Teacher-of-the-Year, not Teacher-of-the-Half-Year."

"That's what I thought. She would have to stay to win."

"Hmmmmmmm," Kate said waving the letter. "This is good . . . but . . ."

"But what?" John asked.

"I don't know if it's good enough."

John sighed. His own hope was also mixed with doubt.

"It won't hurt to try," he whispered, shoving the letter into Mr. Dillard's box. "Besides, things can't get any worse."

That's when they heard a knock at the door.

CHAPTER 7

Trapped in the Restroom

Kate and John froze.

"So you weren't doing a thing, Buzzy." Mrs. Washburn's voice was loud and clear outside the door.

"N-n-no," Buzzy stuttered.

"You were just standing in the hall minding your own business."

"Yes ma'am. Just minding my own business."

"Right in front of the teachers' lounge," she continued.

"Yes, right in front of the . . ." Buzzy stopped before revealing his friends' location.

"Teachers' lounge," Mrs. Washburn finished.

"Maybe we need to take a look inside the lounge."

Kate grabbed John's arm.

"Quick! In the restroom."

Kate and John closed the restroom door just as the door to the lounge opened. They heard the squeak of tennis shoes coming into the room.

"Let's look around," Mrs. Washburn said.

They heard her walking around the room. She stopped in front of the restroom. John could see her shadow under the door. He held his breath. He and Kate were like the ants trapped in tunnels after the earthquake—only they couldn't dig their way out. At this moment they didn't want out. The outside world held danger, Mrs. Washburn.

"Buzzy, I have some advice for you." Mrs. Washburn rocked back and forth on her tennis shoes. Squeak. Squeak. "If you don't give me any trouble." Squeak. Squeak. "Then I won't give you any trouble."

"No ma'am. No trouble at all. I never give trouble, not if I can help it. And I know I would never give YOU any trou . . ."

"All right, Buzzy," she said. "Get back to your

class. And I don't want to see you in the hall again."

"Yes ma'am."

Even after they heard the door close behind Buzzy and Mrs. Washburn, John and Kate didn't move. Neither of them trusted Mrs. Washburn. She could be waiting outside, ready to pounce.

Kate mouthed the words. "Do you think she's gone?"

John nodded. He wasn't nervous about Mrs. Washburn anymore. He had a different feeling. It was embarrassment. Suddenly he was aware that he was in the restroom with a girl. They were standing there having a conversation with a toilet between them. He had not noticed the toilet before, but now it seemed like the biggest thing in the room.

Mrs. Washburn or no Mrs. Washburn, John had to get out of that restroom. John reached for the doorknob and quickly stepped outside. He couldn't be caught in there with Kate.

He could imagine the other students asking him, "Why do you have detention, John?"

"Because I was in the restroom with Kate."

John turned red just thinking about it.

Kate didn't seem to notice.

"Let's get back to class," she said.

"Yes," John said with a sigh of relief. "Let's get as far away from here as possible."

CHAPTER 8

Ant Talk

Thursday morning John, Buzzy, and Kate walked down the hall toward their classroom.

"So, how is Big Jim?" Buzzy asked.

"Great," John answered. "When I left this morning he was talking to two workers."

"Talking?" asked Kate.

"They talk by tapping their antennae together," Buzzy explained.

"Did they get everything cleaned up?" Buzzy asked.

"Almost," John said. "I think by tomorrow earthquake recovery should be complete."

"That's amazing. I didn't think it would be that quick," Buzzy said as they rounded the corner and walked into the classroom.

The three friends stopped suddenly and stood speechless. There was a frenzy of activity inside.

Three girls followed one another up and down the aisles, putting a napkin and cup at each desk. Just like the ants following each other through the tunnels, thought John.

He watched two boys hanging crepe paper. One stood in the middle cutting and taping. The other carried the ends to their final locations. It reminded John of Digger, who had stayed in the lower chamber digging while another ant carried the sand away.

There was even a large trash can at the front of the room.

"The refuse pile," John mumbled.

"What?" Kate asked.

"Oh nothing," John said.

Kate pointed to the room. "This is not what I wanted."

John shrugged. "An earthquake was not what the ants wanted either."

Buzzy nodded. "But the ants are recovering."

"How?" asked Kate.

"They kept working," Buzzy answered.

John nodded. "Yeah, Digger and Pea Brain couldn't see what was ahead of them, but they kept digging anyway."

"Digging?" asked Kate.

"Yes," said John. "And everything turned out great."

Mrs. Lucas came up to them. "I'm so glad you three are here," she said. "It's important to say goodbye to people who are special to you."

Mrs. Lucas looked at each of them in turn. "Goodbye is more than an ending. It marks a beginning. One good thing ends, and another begins."

"Sometimes you don't know when the next good thing is going to come," John said.

"But you keep going anyway," Mrs. Lucas said. She smiled. "If there were an award for Students of the Year I would nominate the three of you."

She gave them each a hug.

John looked into the classroom, where the children were laughing and talking. He turned to Buzzy and Kate. "Let's start digging."

CHAPTER 9

The Mysterious Box

Friday morning there was a large cardboard box on Mrs. Lucas' desk. Everyone was whispering quietly. The new teacher had not arrived yet.

"I saw it move," Kate whispered.

"Boxes don't move by themselves," Buzzy said.

"That one did," Kate insisted. "I saw it with my own eyes."

"Well," Buzzy said. "Your eyes are worse than my mother's."

"Then what do you think it is, mushbrain?" Kate asked.

"I don't know," Buzzy answered, frowning. "Probably books."

John was sure it was not books. Kate was

right, the box had moved. It was only a slight move, but a move nonetheless. John was sure of that.

"Go look," Kate said to John.

"Why don't you look?" he shot back. The thought was like a hot potato. He wanted to get rid of it quickly. In his mind was a vivid picture of Mrs. Washburn standing in the teachers' lounge by the restroom door. It had been too close for comfort. John didn't want to get caught doing anything he wasn't supposed to do.

"Just pretend you're going to sharpen your pencil," Kate said, "and see if the box has a top. Just look, that's all."

"I probably shouldn't," John said. He had not taken his eyes off of the box since it moved. Then, without another word, John picked up his pencil and headed for the front of the class-room.

"He's going to look," Kate announced.

"Be careful," someone yelled.

All eyes were on John. When he got to the box he stopped.

"Go ahead," someone yelled.

John stood on tiptoes to see over the top of

the box. He felt like an ant inspecting a new item of food.

"It has a top and it's shut," he reported in a loud whisper. He was ready to go back to his desk when he heard a scratching noise from inside the box. He jumped.

"Look. It moved," someone yelled. "Did you see it? It moved again."

"Open it," someone yelled from the back.

John looked at the door. There was no sign of anyone coming. He looked back at the box. The scratching had stopped.

To open the box he would have to stand on the teacher's chair. That was the only way to reach the top of the box. John could not explain in a million years why he did it, but he climbed up onto the teacher's chair.

"He's going to open it," Kate announced. She wiggled nervously in her seat.

John examined the top.

"It's taped closed," he reported.

"Go ahead," someone yelled. "Pull the tape off." It sounded like Buzzy.

John grabbed the tape. He was ready to pull when the door to the classroom opened and in walked a tall, skinny man wearing a sweater. John froze. Everyone in the class took a deep breath. John was sure they had sucked all the air out of the room, because suddenly he couldn't breathe.

CHAPTER 10

Hello, Mr. C

"**A**h, I see you've found my box," the man said, smiling. John stood on the chair with his arms at his sides. He felt like a statue in the park, high up on a pedestal for everyone to see.

"Stay right there, young man, because I need someone to help me unpack my box. In fact, I need two people."

Buzzy's hand shot up. The man pointed to Buzzy, who was already on his way to the front.

"This is a most important box," the skinny man said, as though he had known them all year. "In it I have my most important teaching items."

John could see Kate's lips silently form the word books.

"No, young lady, it's not books. What is your name?"

"Kate," she said loudly.

"Books is a very good guess, Kate. They are important for learning. But this box does not contain books. Why don't you come help these boys unpack my box?"

Kate walked slowly to the front and stood beside Buzzy.

"By the way, class, I'm Mr. Cunningham, your new teacher." His voice was louder than Kate's. "You can call me Mr. C."

He turned to John. "What's your name?"

John took a deep breath. "John."

"John, I want you to open the box."

As John pulled the tape off, the scratching sound started again. He paused.

"Go ahead," Mr. C said, waving his hand.

John folded back the top and a familiar aroma escaped the box.

"Good morning, Goliath," Mr. C said, pulling out a cage holding a large guinea pig. Goliath scurried around the cage.

"Who can bring in a carrot for Goliath?"

"I can," Kate said.

He handed the cage to Kate.

Next came some goldfish. Then two turtles.

"Can anyone bring lettuce tomorrow for Jack and Jill?" Mr. C asked.

Five hands went up.

Everyone watched as Mr. C removed a box of dirt with earthworms crawling on the top.

"Spike Jones and the City Slickers," he said and put them on the desk.

"Now," Mr. C said. "I must be very careful with this last group." He reached into the bottom of the box. "Because they work very hard."

Carefully, he lifted a large ant farm from the box.

"I need someone to help with this ant farm. Someone with a real interest in their work."

John spoke quickly. "Buzzy will do it."

"How about it, Buzzy?" Mr. C asked. "You interested?"

"And how!" Buzzy said, grinning broadly.

"Careful," Mr. C said. "Ants don't like earthquakes."

John, Buzzy, and Kate looked at Mr. C and smiled. "Nobody does," they said together.